For Linda, Samantha, and Amy
S. G.

For Emmett and Seamus
C. T.

Text copyright © 2000 by Sally Grindley
Illustrations copyright © 2000 by Carol Thompson

First U.S. edition 2000

Library of Congress Cataloging-in-Publication Data

Grindley, Sally.
A new room for William / Sally Grindley ; illustrated by Carol Thompson.
p. cm.
Summary: When William and his mother move, he is unhappy about having a new room,
but he changes his mind after he gets dinosaur wallpaper and makes a new friend.
ISBN 0-7636-1196-4
[1. Bedrooms—Fiction. 2. Moving, Household—Fiction. 3. Divorce—Fiction.] I. Thompson, Carol, ill. II. Title.
PZ7.G88446 Ne 2000
[E]—dc21 99-054315

2 4 6 8 10 9 7 5 3 1

Printed in Hong Kong/China

This book was typeset in Calligraphic Bold.
The illustrations were done in mixed media.

Candlewick Press
2067 Massachusetts Avenue
Cambridge, Massachusetts 02140

A New Room for William

Sally Grindley illustrated by Carol Thompson

CANDLEWICK PRESS

CAMBRIDGE, MASSACHUSETTS

William walked into his room in the new house and made a face.

"I like my old room better," he said.

His old room had posters on the walls and shelves crammed with toys.

His old room had a soft red carpet and bright yellow curtains. This room was bare except for his bed and a pile of boxes.

"Just wait and see," said Mom. "When *we're* done, you're going to love it."

William looked out the window. From his old room he could see his jungle gym and the place where he and Dad had a garden. All he could see from this room were weeds, laundry, a big old tree— and a boy waving! William didn't wave back.

That night, William could not sleep. He was used to the shapes in his old room—his bathrobe that looked like a gorilla and his lampshade that looked like a pirate's hat. But here the moon threw ghostly shadows through the bare windows. William hid under the covers.

"I want to go back to our old house," he cried, when Mom came to check on him.

The next day, Mom took William shopping.

"Let's choose some wallpaper for your room," she said.

"I want the same paper I had in my old room," said William.

"That's fine," said Mom. "But let's look anyway. You might find one you like better."

William looked and found the paper that he had in his old room. He was about to choose it when he saw a dinosaur staring at him from another paper. William liked dinosaurs.

"This one," he said suddenly. "I like this one."

When they went home, William rushed upstairs to his room and began to rummage through one of the boxes.

He pulled out a toy dinosaur, and another, and another, then stood them in a row on the windowsill. The boy next door waved at him again. William waved back shyly and stomped his dinosaurs around.

That night, William watched the moon throw ghostly shadows through the bare windows, and he turned them all into dinosaurs.

"When will my new room be ready?" he asked, when Mom came to check on him.

"I'll start in the morning," said Mom, "and you can help."

William woke up bright and early.

"Can we start now?" he asked, as soon as he jumped out of bed.

"Can we start now?" he asked, as soon as he finished breakfast.

Mom let him stir the wallpaper paste. "Yuck! It's all slimy!" said William. Then he held the ladder while Mom climbed up.

"Keep it steady, William!" she said.

Little by little, William's room began to change, as more and more dinosaurs covered the walls.

"They're chasing each other, Mom!" cried William, and he ran around the room, pretending to be a dinosaur.

Then he ran out to the yard and galloped along the path.

"GRRRR!" he growled. "I'm a fierce dinosaur."

"RAARRR!" came a voice. "I'm an even fiercer dinosaur."

Upside down in the big old tree was the boy from next door.

"Hello," said the boy. "I'm Tom."

"I'm getting a new room," said William proudly.

"Can I see it?" asked Tom.

"It's not finished yet," said William.

grrrr

William climbed the tree and sat next
to Tom.

"We can share this tree," said Tom.
"Some of it's in my yard and some of
it's in yours."

William looked down into Tom's
yard. There was a jungle gym, just like
the one he used to have at his old
house. For a moment he felt sad again.

"I had to leave my jungle gym
behind," he said.

"Let's play on mine," said Tom.

William clambered and scrambled and chased his new friend. What did it matter that this jungle gym was in Tom's yard and not his? Jungle gyms were only fun if you had someone to play with, and he didn't have a friend next door at his old house.

Suddenly, Mom opened a window and called, "William, come and see your room now."

"Come on, Tom," said William, excitedly. "Come and see my new room!"

William couldn't believe his eyes when he opened the door.

"Thank you, Mom," he said, and he galloped around in circles.

"Lucky you," said Tom, and he galloped around behind him.

That night, William snuggled down with his favorite toy animals and looked around his new room. The moon shone brightly through the new curtains and picked out a Tyrannosaurus rex chasing a Stegosaurus. William smiled.

When Mom came in to check on him, he said, "Will Dad let me choose the paper for my room at his new house?"

"I'm sure he will," said Mom. "Sleep tight now."

And William did.